HISTORY SPEAKS

PICTURE BOOKS PLUS READER'S THEATER

Johnny Moore and the WRIGHT BROTHERS' FLYING MACHINE

BY **WALTER A. SCHULZ**

ILLUSTRATED BY **DOUG BOWLES**

M MILLBROOK PRESS / MINNEAPOLIS

To my family, to my friends at Lerner Publishing, and a special thanks to Dana Bowles and to Jackson "Johnny Moore" Merckens —DB

Text and illustrations copyright © 2011 by Lerner Publishing Group, Inc.

Millbrook Press
A division of Lerner Publishing Group, Inc.
241 First Avenue North
Minneapolis, MN 55401 U.S.A.

Website address: www.lernerbooks.com

The images in this book are used with the permission of:
Library of Congress pp. 32 (LC-DIG-ppprs-00626), 33 (LC-USZ62-6166A).

Library of Congress Cataloging-in-Publication Data

Schulz, Walter A.
     Johnny Moore and the Wright brothers' flying machine / by Walter A.
  Schulz ; illustrated by Doug Bowles.
        p.   cm. — (History speaks: picture books plus reader's theater)
     Includes bibliographical references.
     ISBN 978-0-7613-5876-3 (lib. bdg. : alk. paper)
     1. Wright, Orville, 1871–1948—Juvenile literature. 2. Wright, Wilbur, 1867–
  1912—Juvenile literature. 3. Aeronautics—United States—History—Juvenile
  literature. 4. Moore, Johnny—Juvenile literature. 5. Wright *Flyer* (Airplane)—
  Juvenile literature. I. Bowles, Doug. II. Title.
  TL540.W7S379 2011
  973—dc22   2010021589

Manufactured in the United States of America
1 – CG – 12/31/10

CONTENTS

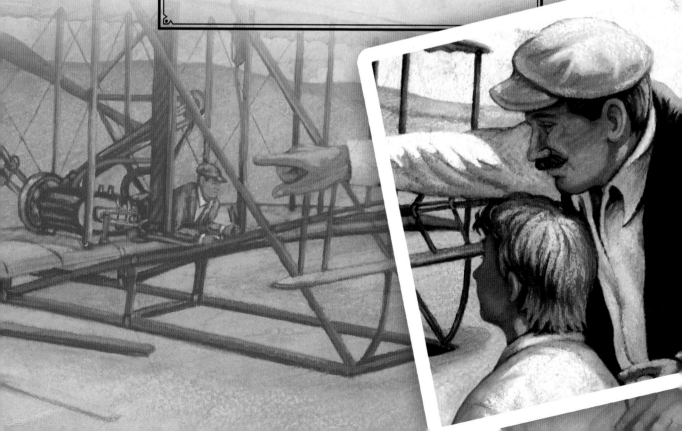

KITTY HAWK, NORTH CAROLINA

December 17, 1903

Johnny Moore looked out the window. Large white clouds filled the sky. The wind was blowing so hard that the roof shook.

"Be no fishing today," his mother said.

Johnny groaned to himself. Another slow day of fixing fishnets and doing chores. His mother smiled.

"How about bringing some fish to the men at the lifesaving station?" she asked.

Johnny jumped up.
"I'll be back early!"
He put on his coat. Then he ran along the beach.
Big waves crashed upon the shore.

Johnny lived on one of the sandy islands off North
Carolina called the Outer Banks. The islands could
be very dangerous. Every year, bad weather wrecked
many of the ships that passed by.

The people at the lifesaving stations rescued sailors from sinking ships. Johnny liked to visit the brave men who lived at the station close to the village of Kitty Hawk. But most of all, he liked to watch the Wright brothers, Wilbur and Orville. The brothers lived at the bottom of a big hill near the lifesaving station. They flew down the hill on big gliders.

For three summers, Will and Orv had come to North Carolina from Ohio. The Outer Banks was dangerous for ships. But it was the best place for the brothers to test their gliders, machines that flew on the wind. The wind blew every day. The sand was soft. There were no trees or rocks to run into!

Many people in the nearby villages thought Will and Orv were crazy. Johnny thought they were very smart. Once Johnny heard people talking about Will and Orv. Johnny told them, "I saw Will fly down the hill just like a bird!"

One of the women said, "A bird can fly wherever it wants. A bird can fly right off the ground. It doesn't need a hill to jump off." They all laughed except Johnny.

Once Johnny saw the strangest thing when he visited Will and Orv. The brothers were putting a motor on a big glider. They called this glider a flying machine. They named it *Flyer*.

This year, Will and Orv hadn't gone home at the end of the summer. They stayed so that they could test the *Flyer*. Will and Orv told Johnny that no one had ever flown into the sky using a motor on a flying machine. Just the thought of flying made Johnny's heart thump. Going down the hill on a glider was exciting. But flying up with the birds was scary. What if the motor stopped? Or one of the wings broke?

The wind was still blowing when Johnny reached
the lifesaving station. He opened the door.
  "Hello, Johnny," said Mr. Daniels. "I see you've
brought us some fish."
  Johnny sat at the long table.

"The other day, Will and Orv tried to fly their machine,"
Mr. Daniels said.

"You mean the one with the motor?" asked Johnny.

"Yup," Mr. Daniels said. "But it didn't work. The machine
made a big bounce and then smacked into the sand.
Those propellers were spinning fast. You couldn't even
see them turning!"

"Propellers?" Johnny asked.

"The motor turns two big spinning blades. They push
the glider up into the sky," said Mr. Daniels.

Johnny was amazed.

"Will and Orv must be the bravest people in the world!" said Johnny.

"That's for sure. Other people tried the same thing with a flying machine. But it crashed right into a river," Mr. Daniels said as he shook his head.

Just then, they heard a voice yell from the lookout tower. Mr. Westcott called down, "The flag is up! Will and Orv are going to try out their flying machine again!" Johnny jumped up from the table. The flag was a signal. It meant that the brothers needed help with one of their machines. Four of the men left quickly. Johnny ran to keep up.

As they reached the first shed, Orv came out. He had on a stiff collar and a tie. The brothers always dressed up.

"Hello, boys," Orv said. "Great day for flying."

One of the men answered, "The wind is blowing too hard. It's a great day for breaking your neck!"

"We can't wait any longer," Orv said. "The weather is turning bad. We're already months late in testing the *Flyer*."

Johnny thought about that other flying machine that had crashed. He looked up and saw a seagull. It was trying to fly into the wind. If a bird was having a hard time, how could Will and Orv fly? He didn't want his friends to get hurt.

Will came out of the shed. "The wind is blowing hard—more than twenty-five miles an hour, Orv," he said. He looked very worried.

Orv looked up at the gray sky.

"This is our day, Will. Today is our day to finally fly!" said Orv.

He opened the big doors on the second shed. Inside in the dark sat the *Flyer*. It was much bigger than the gliders. But the flying machine didn't look very strong. The *Flyer* seemed to be made of matchsticks and cloth. Johnny saw the motor on the bottom wing. The two propellers were behind the wings.

Will climbed onto the *Flyer*. He lay down on his stomach on a flat piece of wood. He was right next to the motor. Wires leading to the wings were attached to the boards he was lying on. When Will moved the boards from side to side, the wings twisted and changed shape.

"This is the secret to flying, Johnny," Will said. "Other people have flown on gliders. But this flying machine can change directions. Whenever I move, the wings twist just like a bird's."

Orv turned to Johnny. "Look at the motor we built," he said. "It's as strong as eight horses."

Johnny was speechless. He didn't believe that the little engine could be as powerful as even one horse.

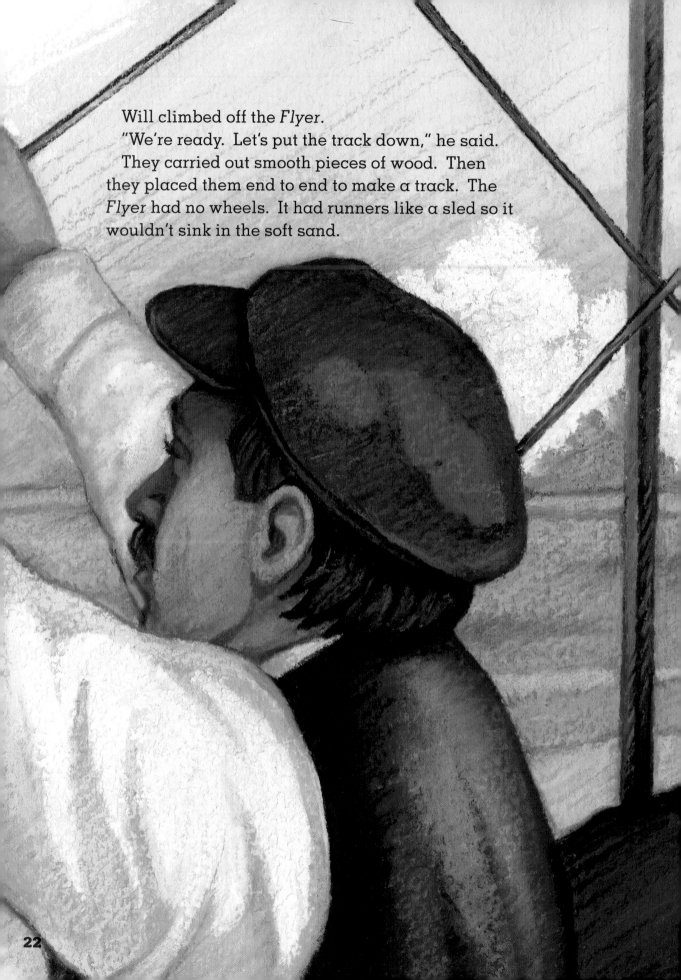

Will climbed off the *Flyer*.
"We're ready. Let's put the track down," he said.
They carried out smooth pieces of wood. Then
they placed them end to end to make a track. The
Flyer had no wheels. It had runners like a sled so it
wouldn't sink in the soft sand.

Johnny helped hold the *Flyer* on the track.
The wind almost lifted it up. Johnny and the
others held on with all their might. Orv
climbed onto the machine. He lay down on
the wood near the middle of the wing.
He turned his hat around so it
wouldn't blow off.

23

Then he gave the signal to Will.

"Come on, boys!" yelled Will. "Let's give a cheer for Orv. No one has ever flown off flat ground using a motor!"

Will began to spin one of the propellers.

jumped at the noise. Black smoke shot out of a pipe. The *Flyer* started to shake. It seemed about to fall apart. Johnny looked at the others holding on to the *Flyer*. Everyone looked frightened. Orv turned to Johnny. He smiled and signaled to let go. Johnny let go of the wing.

Orv let loose of the wire that held the machine to the track. The *Flyer* started to move slowly. Will held one wing and started to walk along with the *Flyer*. Soon he was running. The *Flyer* quickly picked up speed. Will finally let go.

"IT'S UP!"

The *Flyer* had lifted up off the track. It flew right into the wind. The flying machine rose up and then plunged down into the sand. Johnny was scared. Everyone began to run.

Orv lay very still on the wing. The motor was running. The propellers continued to spin.

"Orv, are you all right?" yelled Will.

No answer. Finally, Orv moved. He reached over and turned off the motor. Slowly, he stood up. Orv stepped down onto the ground. He brushed the sand from his face.

"I guess we sure flew today, Will. How long was the flight?" Orv said with a big smile.

"Twelve seconds. And over 120 feet!" shouted Will.

The two brothers happily shook hands. Will turned to the helpers and said, "You are the official witnesses to the first powered flight. A flying machine with a person on it took off on its own power. And it flew under control!"

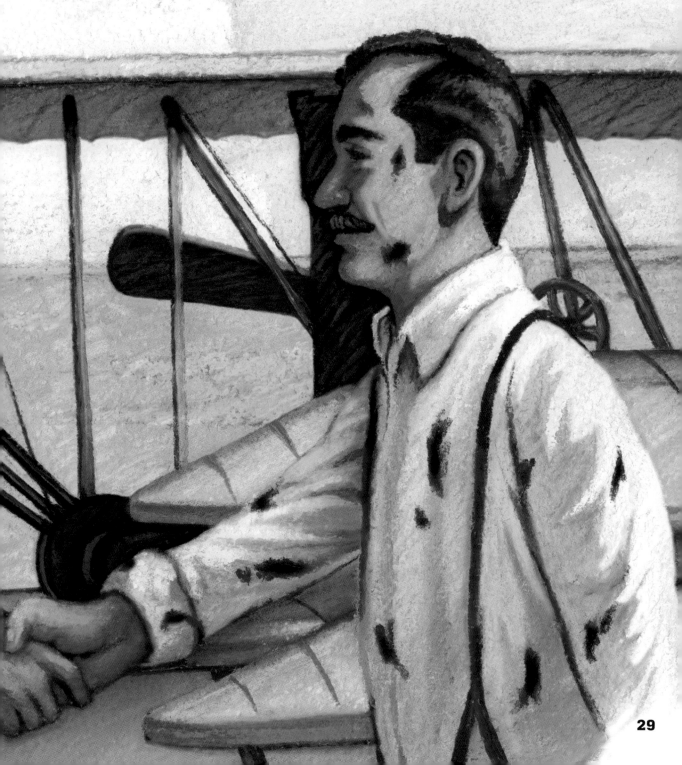

Orv looked at Johnny. "What you saw has never been done before. We are the first. We couldn't have done it without help from you and the others. Always remember December 17, 1903."

The *Flyer* flew three more times that morning. The brothers took turns. Will stayed up almost a minute. He traveled over 850 feet.

Walking back home, Johnny knew Orv was right. He would never forget this day. Seagulls were flying over his head. Johnny knew now that people could fly just like birds.

Author's Note

The events that took place on December 17, 1903, when Wilbur and Orville Wright first flew an aircraft with a motor, changed the history of the world. The Wright brothers made many parts of their flying machine at their bicycle shop in Dayton, Ohio. Then they tested their ideas on the sand dunes of Kitty Hawk, North Carolina.

Until Wilbur and Orville brought together the necessary ideas, no one in history had ever built a machine that could take off from level ground and fly. The brothers did not invent human flight, but they developed the method to enable the first engine-powered aircraft to go up, down, and turn. Wilbur and Orville made all the parts by hand and even built the engine for the craft they named *Flyer*.

Johnny Moore and the Wright Brothers' Flying Machine is based on historical records of that windy December day long

WILBUR AND ORVILLE WRIGHT, 1909

THE FIRST POWERED FLIGHT AT KITTY HAWK, DECEMBER 17, 1903

ago. The words spoken by the characters in the story were invented by the author to bring life to the event. There were five people who witnessed the first flight of the *Flyer*. Four men were from the nearby lifesaving station, and the other is identified as "young Johnny Moore of Nags Head."

Performing Reader's Theater

Dear Student,

Reader's Theater is a dramatic reading. It is a little like a play, but you don't need to memorize your lines. Here are some tips that will help you do your best in a Reader's Theater performance.

BEFORE THE PERFORMANCE

- **Choose your part:** Your teacher may assign parts, or you may be allowed to choose your own part. The character you play does not need to be the same age as you. A boy can play the part of a girl, and a girl can play the part of a boy. That's why it's called acting!

- **Find your lines:** Your character's name is always the same color. The name at the bottom of each page tells you which character has the first line on the next page. If you are allowed to write on your script, highlight your lines. If you cannot write on the script, you may want to use sticky flags to mark your lines.

- **Check pronunciations of words:** If your character's lines include any words you aren't sure how to pronounce, check the pronunciation guide on page 45. If a word isn't there or you still aren't sure how to say it, check a dictionary or ask a teacher, librarian, or other adult.

- **Use your emotions:** Think about how your character feels in the story. If you imagine how your character feels, the audience will hear the emotion in your voice.

- **Use your imagination:** Think about how your character's voice might sound. For example, an old man's voice will sound different from a baby's voice. If you do change your voice, make sure the audience can still understand the words you are saying.

- **Practice your lines:** Even though you do not need to memorize your lines, you should still be comfortable reading them. Read your lines aloud often so they flow smoothly.

DURING THE PERFORMANCE

- **Keep your script away from your face but high enough to read:** If you cover your face with your script, you block your voice from the audience. If you have your script too low, you need to tip your head down farther to read it and the audience won't be able to hear you.

- **Use eye contact:** Good Reader's Theater performers look at the audience as much as they look at their scripts. If you look down, the sound of your voice goes down to the script and not out to the audience.

- **Speak clearly:** Make sure you are loud enough. Say all your words carefully. Be sure not to read too quickly. Remember, if you feel nervous, you may start to speak faster than usual.

- **Use facial expressions and gestures:** Your facial expressions and gestures (hand movements) help the audience know how your character is feeling. If your character is happy, smile. If your character is angry, cross your arms and be sure not to smile.

- **Have fun:** It's okay if you feel nervous. If you make a mistake, just try to relax and keep going. Reader's Theater is meant to be fun for the actors and the audience!

Cast of Characters

NARRATOR 1

NARRATOR 2

NARRATOR 3

JOHNNY MOORE

ORVILLE WRIGHT (ORV)

WILBUR WRIGHT (WILL)

READER 1:
Mrs. Moore, townsperson

READER 2:
Mr. Daniels, Mr. Westcott

SOUND:
This part has no lines. The person in this role
is in charge of the sound effects.
Find the sound effects for this script
at www.lerneresource.com.

The Script

NARRATOR 1: Johnny Moore looked out the window. Large white clouds filled the skies of Kitty Hawk, North Carolina. The wind was blowing so hard that the roof shook.

READER 1 (as Mrs. Moore): Be no fishing today, Johnny.

NARRATOR 2: Johnny groaned.

JOHNNY: Another slow day of fixing fishnets and doing chores.

NARRATOR 2: His mother smiled.

READER 1 (as Mrs. Moore): How about bringing some fish to the men at the lifesaving station?

NARRATOR 3: Johnny jumped up.

JOHNNY: I'll be back early!

NARRATOR 3: He put on his coat. Then he ran along the beach. Big waves crashed upon the shore.

NARRATOR 1: Johnny lived on one of the sandy islands of the Outer Banks off North Carolina. The islands could be very dangerous. Every year, bad weather wrecked many of the ships that passed by.

NARRATOR 2: The people at the lifesaving stations rescued sailors from sinking ships. Johnny liked to visit the brave men who lived at the station. But most of all, he liked to watch the Wright brothers, Wilbur and Orville.

Next Page — **NARRATOR 3**

NARRATOR 3: The brothers lived at the bottom of a big hill near the station. They flew down the hill on big gliders, machines that flew on the wind. For three summers, Will and Orv had come to North Carolina from Ohio.

NARRATOR 1: The Outer Banks was dangerous for ships. But it was the best place for the brothers to test their gliders. The wind blew every day. The sand was soft. There were no trees to run into!

NARRATOR 2: Many people in the nearby villages thought Will and Orv were crazy. Johnny thought they were very smart. Once Johnny heard people joking about Will and Orv.

JOHNNY: I saw Will fly down the hill just like a bird!

READER 1 (as townsperson): A bird can fly wherever it wants. A bird can fly right off the ground. It doesn't need a hill to jump off.

NARRATOR 3: They all laughed except Johnny.

SOUND: [crowd laughing]

NARRATOR 1: Once Johnny saw the strangest thing when he visited Will and Orv. The brothers were putting a motor on a big glider. They called this glider a flying machine. They named it *Flyer*.

NARRATOR 2: This year, Will and Orv hadn't gone home at the end of the summer. They stayed so that they could test the *Flyer*. No one had ever flown into the sky using a motor on a flying machine.

Next Page — **NARRATOR 3**

NARRATOR 3: Just the thought of flying made Johnny's heart thump. Going down the hill on a glider was exciting. But flying up with the birds was scary.

JOHNNY: What if the motor stops? Or one of the wings breaks?

SOUND: [gusts of wind]

NARRATOR 1: The wind was still blowing when Johnny reached the lifesaving station. Mr. Daniels opened the door.

READER 2 (as Mr. Daniels): Hello, Johnny. I see you've brought us some fish.

NARRATOR 2: Johnny gave him the fish and sat at the long table.

READER 2 (as Mr. Daniels): The other day, Will and Orv tried to fly their machine.

JOHNNY: You mean the one with the motor.

READER 2 (as Mr. Daniels): Yup. But it didn't work. The machine made a big bounce and then smacked into the sand. Those propellers were spinning fast. You couldn't even see them turning!

JOHNNY: Propellers?

READER 2 (as Mr. Daniels): The motor turns two big spinning blades. They push the glider up into the sky.

Next Page — **JOHNNY**

JOHNNY: Will and Orv must be the bravest people in the world!

READER 2 (as Mr. Daniels): That's for sure. Other people tried the same thing with a flying machine. But it crashed right into a river.

NARRATOR 3: Mr. Daniels shook his head. Just then they heard a voice yell from the lookout tower.

READER 2 (as Mr. Westcott): The flag is up! Will and Orv are going to try out their flying machine again!

NARRATOR 1: Johnny jumped up from the table. The flag was a signal. It meant that the brothers needed help with one of their machines. Four of the men left quickly, and Johnny ran to keep up.

NARRATOR 2: As they reached the first shed, Orv came out. He had on a stiff collar and a tie. The brothers always dressed up.

ORV: Hello, boys. Great day for flying.

READER 2 (as Mr. Daniels): The wind is blowing too hard. It's a great day for breaking your neck!

ORV: We can't wait any longer. The weather is turning bad. We're already months late in testing the *Flyer*.

NARRATOR 3: Johnny thought about that other flying machine that had crashed. He looked up and saw a seagull. It was trying to fly into the wind.

SOUND: [seagull call]

Next Page — **JOHNNY**

JOHNNY: If a bird is having a hard time, how can Will and Orv fly? I don't want them to get hurt.

NARRATOR 1: Will came out of the shed.

WILL: The wind is blowing hard—more than twenty-five miles an hour, Orv.

NARRATOR 1: Will looked very worried. Orv looked up at the gray sky.

ORV: This is our day, Will. Today is our day to finally fly!

NARRATOR 2: Orv opened the doors on the second shed. Inside in the dark sat the *Flyer*. It was much bigger than the gliders. But it didn't look very strong.

NARRATOR 3: The *Flyer* seemed to be made of matchsticks and cloth. Johnny saw the motor on the bottom wing. The two propellers were behind the wings.

NARRATOR 1: Will climbed onto the *Flyer*. He lay down on a flat piece of wood. Wires leading to the wings were attached to the boards he was lying on. When Will moved the boards from side to side, the wings twisted and changed shape.

WILL: This is the secret to flying, Johnny. Other people have flown on gliders. But this flying machine can change directions. Whenever I move, the wings twist just like a bird's.

ORV: Look at the motor we built. It's as strong as eight horses.

Next Page — **NARRATOR 2**

NARRATOR 2: Johnny was speechless. He didn't believe that the little engine could be as powerful as even one horse. Will climbed off the *Flyer*.

WILL: We're ready. Let's put the track down.

NARRATOR 3: They carried out smooth pieces of wood. Then they placed them end to end to make a track. The *Flyer* had no wheels. It had runners like a sled so it wouldn't sink in the soft sand.

NARRATOR 1: Johnny helped hold the *Flyer* on the track. The wind almost lifted it up. Johnny and the others held on with all their might. Orv climbed onto the machine. He lay down on the wood. Then he gave the signal to Will.

WILL: Come on, boys! Let's give a cheer for Orv. No one has ever flown off flat ground using a motor!

NARRATOR 2: Will began to spin one of the propellers.

SOUND: [motor revving]

NARRATOR 2: Johnny jumped at the motor's loud roar. Black smoke shot out of a pipe. The *Flyer* started to shake. It seemed as if it might fall apart.

NARRATOR 3: Johnny looked at the others holding on to the *Flyer*. Everyone looked frightened. Orv turned to Johnny. He smiled and signaled to let go. Johnny let go of the wing.

NARRATOR 1: Orv let loose of the wire that held the machine to the track. The *Flyer* started to move slowly. Will held one wing and started to walk along with the *Flyer*.

Next Page — **NARRATOR 2**

NARRATOR 2: Soon Will was running. The *Flyer* quickly picked up speed. He finally let go.

WILL: IT'S UP!

NARRATOR 3: The *Flyer* had lifted up off the track. It flew right into the wind. The flying machine rose up and then plunged down into the sand. Johnny was scared. Everyone began to run.

NARRATOR 1: Orv lay very still on the wing. The motor was running. The propellers continued to spin.

WILL: Orv, are you all right?

NARRATOR 2: There was no answer. Finally, Orv moved. He reached over and turned off the motor.

NARRATOR 3: Slowly, he stood up. He brushed the sand from his face. He spoke with a big smile.

ORV: I guess we sure flew today, Will. How long was the flight?

WILL: Twelve seconds. And over 120 feet!

NARRATOR 1: The two brothers happily shook hands. Will turned to the helpers.

WILL: You are the official witnesses to the first powered flight. A flying machine with a person on it took off on its own power. And it flew under control!

Next Page — **ORV**

ORV: What you saw has never been done before. We couldn't have done it without help from you and the others. Always remember December 17, 1903.

NARRATOR 2: The *Flyer* flew three more times that morning. The brothers took turns. Will traveled over 850 feet.

NARRATOR 3: Walking back home, Johnny knew Orv was right. He would never forget this day. Seagulls were flying over his head. Johnny knew now that people could fly just like birds.

Pronunciation Guide

Daniels: DAN-yulz
North Carolina: nohrth kair-uh-LY-nuh
Ohio: oh-HI-oh

Orville Wright: OHR-vull RITE
propellers: proh-PEH-lurz
Wilbur Wright: WIL-buhr RITE
witnesses: WIT-nuhs-sez

Glossary

glider: a motorless aircraft that flies on the wind

groan: a low sound made to express boredom, disagreement, or pain

motor: a machine, usually a type of engine, that allows motion to happen

Outer Banks: a group of narrow islands off the North Carolina coast

propeller: a device with blades that spin to move a larger object forward

seagull: a large, meat-eating bird that usually lives near a coastal area

Selected Bibliography

Chaikin, Andrew. *Air and Space: The National Air and Space Museum Story of Flight*. Boston: Bulfinch Press, 1997.

Kelly, Fred C. *The Wright Brothers: A Biography*. New York: Dover Publications, 1989.

The Papers of Wilbur and Orville Wright: Including the Chanute-Wright Letters. Marvin W. McFarland, Ed. New York: McGraw-Hill, 2001.

Tobin, James. *To Conquer the Air: The Wright Brothers and the Great Race for Flight*. New York: Free Press, 2003.

Wright, Wilbur, Orville Wright, and William J. Claxton. *A History of Early Aviation*. St. Petersburg, FL: Red and Black Publishers, 2009.

Further Reading and Websites

BOOKS

Hill, Lee Sullivan. *The Flyer Flew! The Invention of the Airplane*. Minneapolis: Millbrook Press, 2006.
This book follows the lives of the Wright brothers and the steps they took to build a flying machine. It includes introductions to scientific terms about flight and the research method the Wright brothers used.

O'Brien, Patrick. *Fantastic Flights: One Hundred Years of Flying on the Edge*. New York: Walker & Company, 2003.
Check out seventeen memorable machines, from the Wright brothers' early attempts at flight to *Apollo 11*'s trip to the moon. *Fantastic Flights* also covers famous pilots, including Charles Lindbergh and Amelia Earhart.

Ransom, Candice. *The Lifesaving Adventure of Sam Deal, Shipwreck Rescuer*. Minneapolis: Graphic Universe, 2011.
This graphic novel tells the story of a lifesaving crew on the Outer Banks of North Carolina.

Taylor-Miller, Sandra. *Are We There Yet? The Wright Brothers National Memorial Park*. Boone, NC: Parkway Publishers, 2004.
This book provides information on the historical site where the Wright brothers took flight and suggests activities for park visitors.

Wadsworth, Ginger. *The Wright Brothers*. Minneapolis: Lerner Publications Company, 2004.
Discover the life story of Wilbur and Orville Wright. *The Wright Brothers* features historical photographs, sidebars, color illustrations, and more.

WEBSITES

National Park Service: Wright Brothers National Memorial
http://www.nps.gov/wrbr/index.htm
Learn more about the site where the Wright brothers flew at Kitty Hawk.

Wright Brothers Aeroplane Company
http://www.wright-brothers.org/
Tour this "virtual museum," which has information and photographs about the Wright brothers and the history of American aviation.

Wright Brothers History: U.S. Centennial of Flight Commission
http://www.centennialofflight.gov/wbh/index.htm
This site celebrates the one hundredth anniversary of the flight in Kitty Hawk. It has detailed information and helpful images about the Wright brothers' flying machine and the science behind it.

Dear Teachers and Librarians,

Congratulations on bringing Reader's Theater to your students! Reader's Theater is an excellent way for your students to develop their reading fluency. Phrasing and inflection, two important reading skills, are at the heart of Reader's Theater. Students also develop public speaking skills such as volume, pacing, and facial expression.

The traditional format of Reader's Theater is very simple. There really is no right or wrong way to do it. By following these few tips, you and your students will be ready to explore the world of Reader's Theater.

EQUIPMENT

Location: A theater or gymnasium is a fine place for a Reader's Theater performance, but staging the performance in the classroom works well too.

Scripts: Each reader will need a copy of the script. Scripts that are individually printed should be bound into binders that allow the readers to turn the pages easily. Printable scripts for all the books in this series are available at www.lerneresource.com.

Music Stands: Music stands are very helpful for the readers to set their scripts on.

Costumes: Traditional Reader's Theater does not use costumes. Dressing uniformly, such as all wearing the same color shirt, will give a group a polished look. Specific costume pieces can be used when a reader is performing multiple roles. They help the audience follow the story.

Props: Props are optional. If necessary, readers may mime or gesture to convey objects that are important to the story. Props can be used much like a costume piece to identify different characters performed by one reader. Prop suggestions for each story are available at www.lerneresource.com.

Background and Sound Effects: These aren't essential, but they can add to the fun of Reader's Theater. Customized backgrounds for each story in this series and sound effects corresponding to the scripts are available at www.lerneresource.com. You will need a screen or electronic whiteboard for the background. You will need a computer with speakers to play the sound effects.

PERFORMANCE

Staging: Readers usually face the audience in a straight line or a semicircle. If the readers are using music stands, the stands should be raised chest high. A stand should not block a reader's mouth or face, but it should allow for the reader to read without looking down too much. The main character is usually placed in the center. The narrator is on the end. In the case of multiple narrators, place one narrator on each end.

Reading: Reader's Theater scripts do not need to be memorized. However, the readers should be familiar enough with the script to maintain a fair amount of eye contact with the audience. Encourage readers to act with their voices by reading with inflection and emotion.

Blocking (stage movement): For traditional Reader's Theater, there are no blocking cues to follow. You may want to have the students turn the pages simultaneously. Some groups prefer that readers sit or turn their backs to the audience when their characters are "offstage" or have left a scene. Some groups will have their readers move about the stage, script in hand, to interact with the other readers. The choice is up to you.

Overture and Curtain Call: Before the performance, a member of the group should announce the title and the author of the piece. At the end of the performance, all readers step in front of their music stands, stand in a line, grasp hands, and bow in unison.

Please visit www.lerneresource.com for printable scripts, prop suggestions, sound effects, a background image that can be projected on a screen or electronic whiteboard, a Reader's Theater teacher's guide, and reading-level information for all roles.